The Quarter Note Cowpoke

We would like to thank the following people without whose inspiration or guidance this book would still be words and sketches tossed in a drawer: Charles Lloyd, Michel Petrucciani, Peggy Hitchcock, Brian DeFrees, and Nancy Berger.

Published by Unbroken Circle/Moyer Bell Ltd.

Library of Congress Cataloging-in-Publication Data

Potter, James, 1949-
    The quarter note cowpoke.

    Summary: A boy who likes to play the piano enthusiastically rounds up the musical notes he wants and herds them into the pieces he plays.
    [1. Piano—Fiction. 2. Music—Fiction. 3. Stories in rhyme]
I. Potter, Gale. II. Title.
PZ8.3.P638Qu 1987 [E] 87-5841
ISBN 0-918825-51-2

Design: Jerry Takigawa Design
Printed in Hong Kong by South China Printing Co.
First Edition

The Quarter Note Cowpoke

Words and Pictures by
James and Gale Potter

On a
coral stone cottage
on the south coast
of France,

Lived a
cherub-like boy
playing music
for plants,

And for dogs,
and for cats,
and for bugs,
and for birds,

But especially
for spirits
whose songs
don't use words.

His parents
were puffed up,
near bursting
with pride.

However,
their dreams
and his dreams
did not coincide.

For though Mozart,
Bach
and Beethoven
are fine,

American classics
were what swirled
through his mind.

In his dreams
he's a cowboy
and his bench
is his horse.

The piano he plays?
It's his ranch
why of course!

The notes
that he finds
are like cows
running free.

It's his job
to herd them
to his ranch
"Symphony."

So he plays
as he herds
those cow-notes
in his head,

From the time
the sun wakes him
'til it puts him
to bed.

And
while the sun's sleeping
with the moon
on the rise,

The
quarter note cowpoke
rides watch
in the sky.

So as you saddle up
your dream horse
and ride off to find
the source of starlight,

Remember where
your dreams were born
and keep home always
within heartsight.